Fifi's Fun

Created by Keith Chapman

First published in Great Britain by HarperCollins Children's Books in 2008

1 3 5 7 9 10 8 6 4 2

ISBN-13: 978-0-00-726362-2

ISBN: 0-00-726362-7

Based on the television series *Fifi and the Flowertots* and the original script 'Fifi's Pancake Fun' by Rachel Dawsen.

© Chapman Entertainment Limited 2008

Printed and bound in China

Fifi's Pancake Fun

HarperCollins *Children's Books*

Fifi was busy in her kitchen, making pancakes – and quite a lot of noise! Suddenly there was a ring on the doorbell.

"Hello, Fifi," said Pip. "Do you want to come and play?"
"Not today, Pip – I'm too busy," replied Fifi. "But would you like to help me make some pancakes instead?"
"Yes, please," said Pip. "That sounds like **fun!**"

Fifi showed Pip
how to mix the eggs,
flour and milk together.
"Now where has my
whisk gone?" she asked Pip.
"I only put it down
a moment ago."

Pip giggled. **"Fifi Forget-Me-Not forgot!**
There it is!"

"Thanks, Pip," laughed Fifi. "Now I'll whisk
everything together in the bowl. And then
comes the fun part!"

Over at the Apple Tree House, Stingo was bored.
So he looked through his telescope to see if
anything interesting was going on.
"Hey, Slugsy," he called, "Fifi and Pip are cooking.
Are you hungry?"
"Ssstarving, bosss." sighed Slugsy.

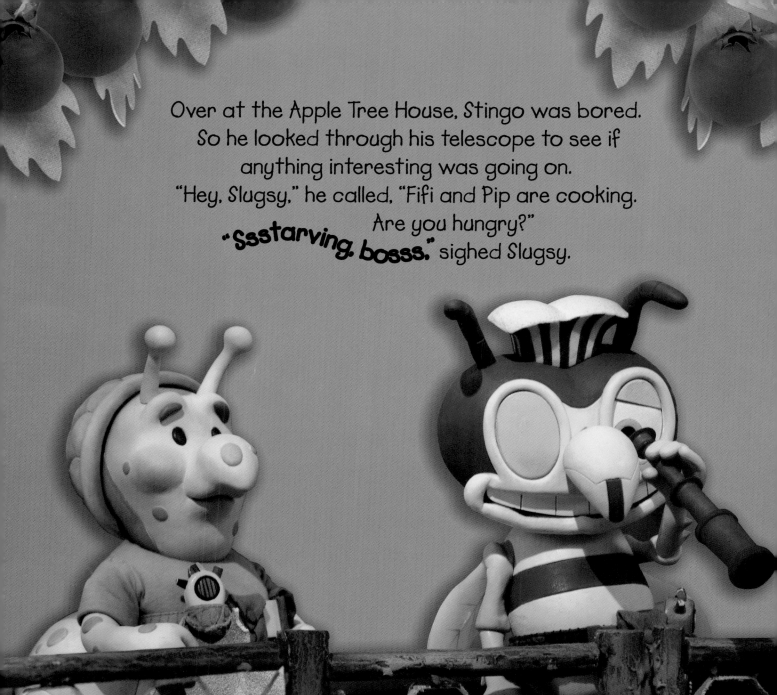

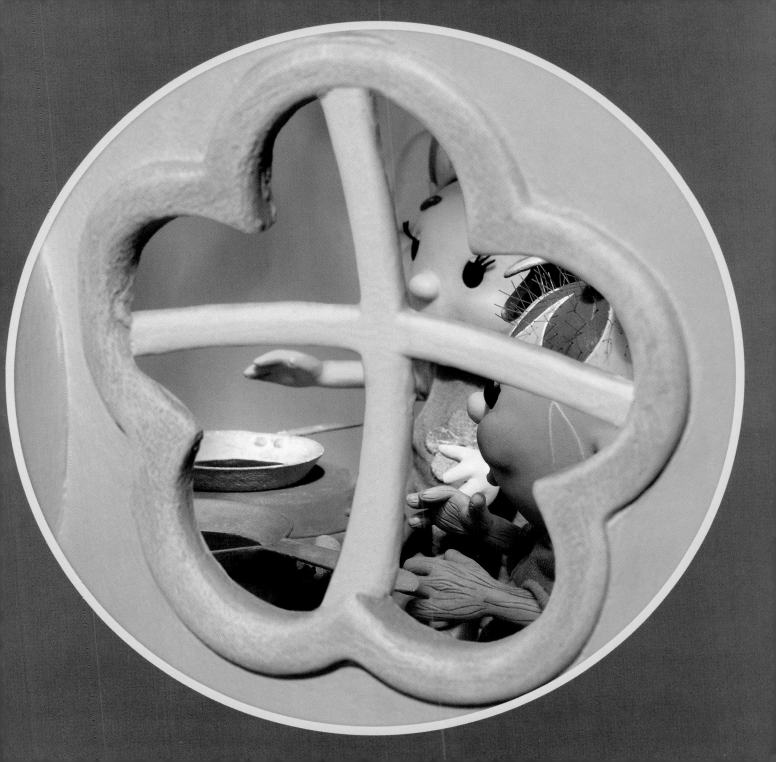

Fifi and Pip had made quite a pile of pancakes, but they were still making more. "Look, bosss," breathed Slugsy, "these are nearly ready..."

"Not quite, Slugsy," buzzed Stingo.
"Pancakes have to be cooked on both sides.
And to do that, they're going to have to flip them!
Which is where we come in..."

Pip's pancakes were flying all over the place. Stingo quickly dashed in and grabbed one of them before it came down.

And Fifi was too busy chasing after her own pancakes to notice! "My pancakes keep falling on the floor, Fifi," said Pip. "And one of them has just disappeared completely!"

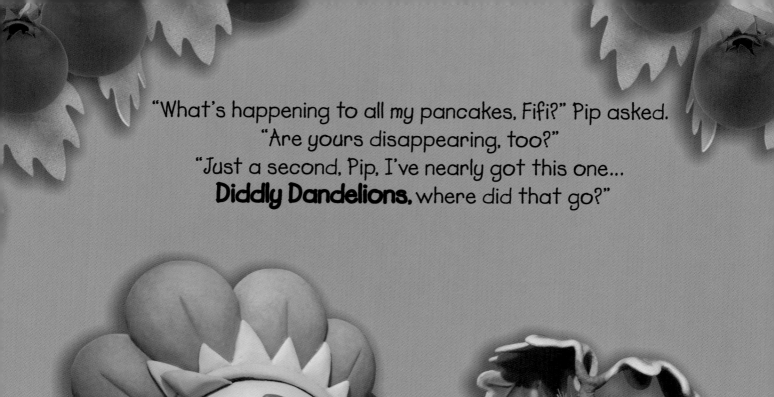

"What's happening to all my pancakes, Fifi?" Pip asked.
"Are yours disappearing, too?"
"Just a second, Pip, I've nearly got this one...
Diddly Dandelions, where did that go?"

One of Fifi's pancakes flew across the room and caught Stingo in the face just as he was about to sneak out.

"Stingo! I might have known!" Fifi sighed.

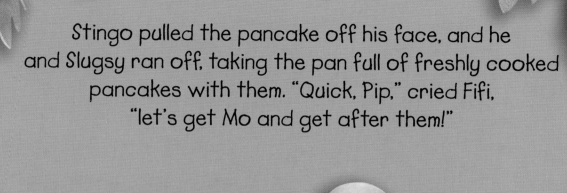

Stingo pulled the pancake off his face, and he
and Slugsy ran off, taking the pan full of freshly cooked
pancakes with them. "Quick, Pip," cried Fifi,
"let's get Mo and get after them!"

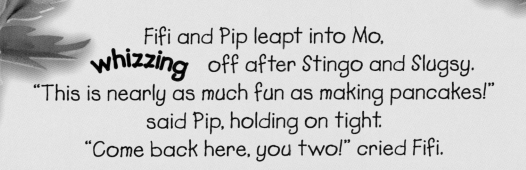

Fifi and Pip leapt into Mo,
whizzing off after Stingo and Slugsy.
"This is nearly as much fun as making pancakes!"
said Pip, holding on tight.
"Come back here, you two!" cried Fifi.

They raced past Poppy's market.
"What's going on, Fifi?" Poppy asked.
"Stingo and Slugsy have stolen
our pancakes," Fifi called.

Stingo looked behind him
to see if Fifi, Pip and Mo
were getting close.
Not looking where he was
going, Stingo bumped into
a tree and dropped the
frying pan!

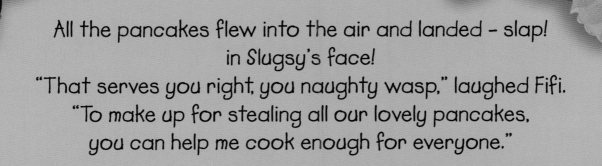

All the pancakes flew into the air and landed – slap!
in Slugsy's face!
"That serves you right, you naughty wasp," laughed Fifi.
"To make up for stealing all our lovely pancakes,
you can help me cook enough for everyone."

And so the Flowertots went to Forget-Me-Not cottage for pancakes. Stingo cooked them properly. He was very good at flipping them.

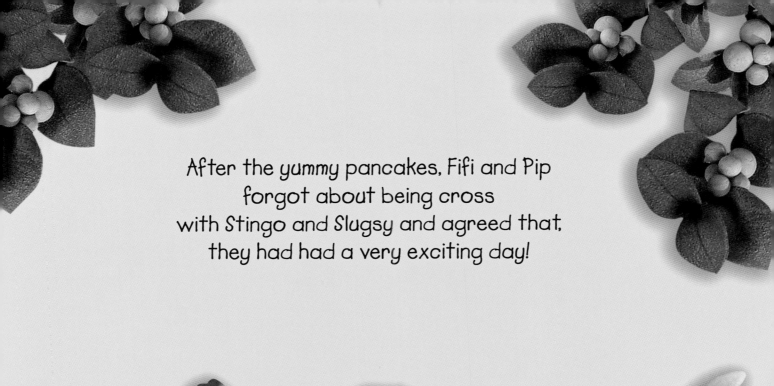

After the *yummy* pancakes, Fifi and Pip
forgot about being cross
with Stingo and Slugsy and agreed that,
they had had a very exciting day!

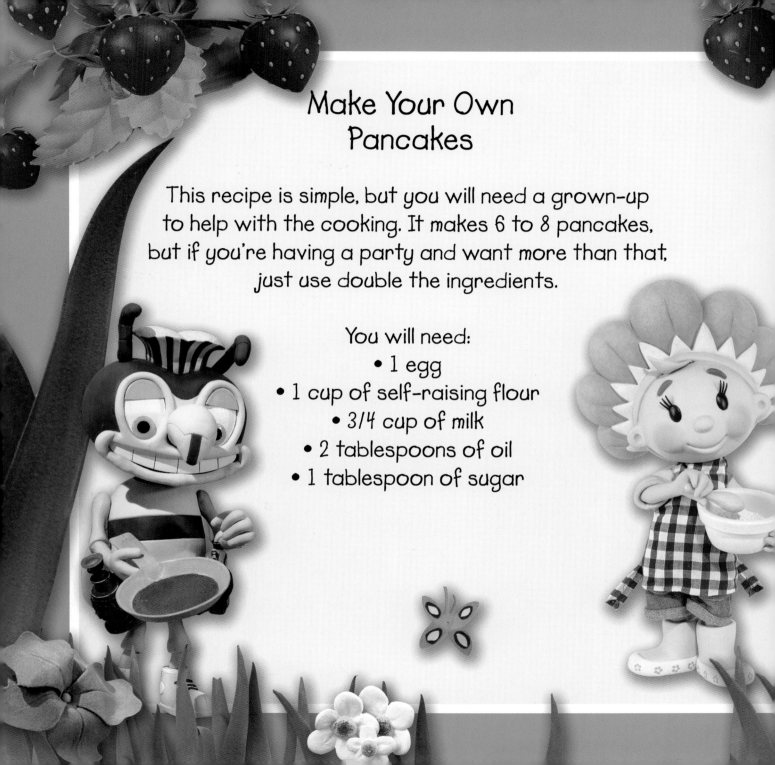

Make Your Own Pancakes

This recipe is simple, but you will need a grown-up to help with the cooking. It makes 6 to 8 pancakes, but if you're having a party and want more than that, just use double the ingredients.

You will need:
- 1 egg
- 1 cup of self-raising flour
- 3/4 cup of milk
- 2 tablespoons of oil
- 1 tablespoon of sugar

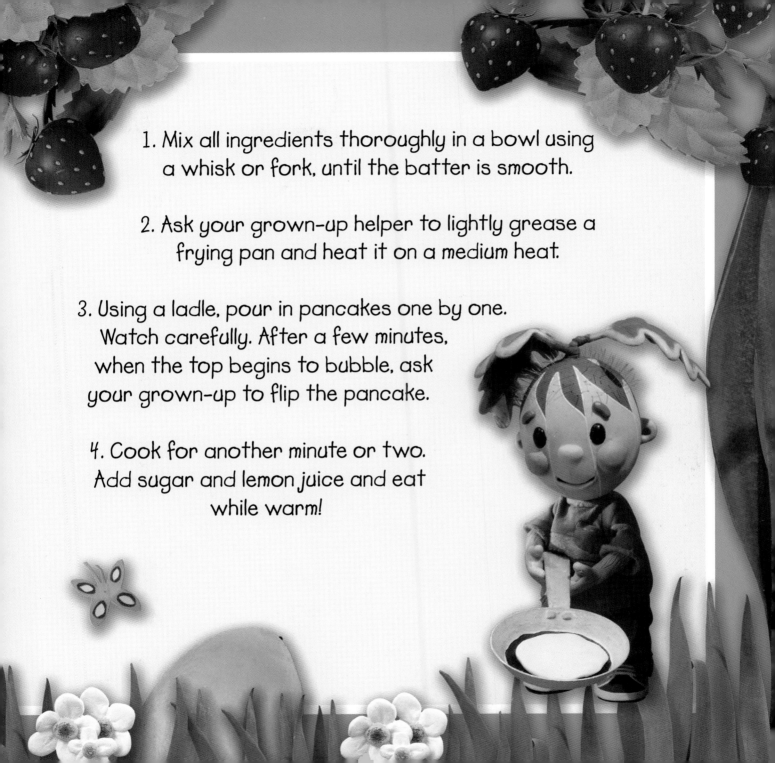

1. Mix all ingredients thoroughly in a bowl using a whisk or fork, until the batter is smooth.

2. Ask your grown-up helper to lightly grease a frying pan and heat it on a medium heat.

3. Using a ladle, pour in pancakes one by one. Watch carefully. After a few minutes, when the top begins to bubble, ask your grown-up to flip the pancake.

4. Cook for another minute or two. Add sugar and lemon juice and eat while warm!